This Little Tiger book belongs to:

_____

_____

_____

_____

For Ian, love always
~ E B

For Levi – our smallest bun
~ J C

LITTLE TIGER PRESS

An imprint of Magi Publications

1 The Coda Centre, 189 Munster Road, London SW6 6AW

www.littletigerpress.com

First published in Great Britain 2007

This edition published 2008

Text copyright © Elizabeth Baguley 2007

Illustrations copyright © Jane Chapman 2007

Elizabeth Baguley and Jane Chapman have asserted their rights to
be identified as the author and illustrator of this work under the Copyright,
Designs and Patents Act, 1988

A CIP catalogue record for this book is available from the British Library

Printed in China

4 6 8 10 9 7 5 3

A Long Way From Home

Elizabeth Baguley   Jane Chapman

LITTLE TIGER PRESS
London

At bedtime in the burrow,
Moz was squished and squashed
by sleepy rabbits.
  "Oh no!" he tutted. "Crumplings!
Move over, Tam."

Tam squeezed over then folded
her arms round Moz, using him
as a hot water bottle.
    "Too hot!" muttered Moz.
"Too many rabbits!"
    So out into the night he went.

"What are you doing out here,
Smallest Bun?" asked Albatross, swooping
down.

"There's no room," snuffled Moz. "And Tam
is always squashing me."

"But she's your favourite sister!"

"It doesn't stop her squashing me," said Moz.

So, to cheer him up, Albatross told Moz
about the land of the North Star, where there
was sky space and snow space.

"No rabbits there!" sighed Moz. "I wish
I could come with you to the frozen North."

"Hop on, then, Smallest Bun," Albatross said.

Moz squeaked as Albatross
lifted into the air.
  Under the moon and
over the wind she flew.
As she soared high, high,
higher, Moz held out his
paws like wings.
  "I'm flying!" he cried.
  "Hold tight! It's the North
Star!" Albatross shouted.

From the North Star
came a wild tornado
of snow and before
Moz could take hold
of Albatross, he had
toppled into the storm.
Swept on the wind he
tumbled and rolled . . .

down . . .

and down . . .

to land *puff!*
in a snowdrift.

Moz was all alone and for a moment he was afraid.
Then he looked around at the empty white space
and shook himself with excitement.
"No squish!" he cried. "No squash!"

Moz danced solo in the snow. He skated
and skimmed and threw snowballs, but
then *whoosh!* he was slipping down an
ice slide, going faster and faster.

Moz skidded to a stop. Oh no!
There were rabbits everywhere!
As he opened his mouth to protest,
the other rabbits did too – but the
only sound was Moz's tiny squeak.

"Mirror rabbits!" he gasped.
These weren't real rabbits,
just reflections in the ice.

Moz was in an ice cave, an ice hall, an ice palace!
It was as big as space and as quiet as silence.
And there was no one there but him.

In the mirror-walls Moz saw himself like a king, his fluff grand with ice crystals.

Moz made a cool, roomy snow-nest.
"No nest-sharings!" he pronounced
and lay royally down to sleep.

When Moz woke, his fluff was frozen and he was cold to the bone. Shivering in his lonely bed, he thought about his snugly sister Tam, squeezed into the nest with all the cosy night-snufflings of his family. Even his tears froze. How he longed to go home!

So, out of the palace he crawled, slipping and slithering up the ice slide until he came out under the open sky where the stony moon shone.

"Albatross!" shouted Moz. "Where are you?"

There was no answer, only the empty creaking of the ice.

But there! A feathery whisper on the wind. Moz looked up and saw wide wings. It was Albatross!

"Smallest Bun!" she said, relieved. "I've been looking for you everywhere!"

She swung Moz on to her back and gratefully he nestled into her warm down, thinking only of home.

Back in the nest, Tam rolled over.
Moz was wonderfully squished and squashed;
he was gorgeously crumpled and crammed.
He was Tam's hot water bottle. He snuggled
into her fluff and, with a sigh, he fell to sleep.

Gillian Lobel
Little Honey Bear and the Smiley Moon
Tim Warnes

cock-a-doodle-hooooooo!
Mick Manning · Brita Granström

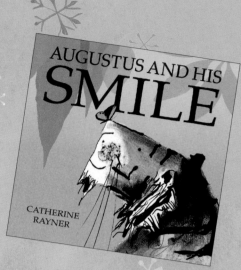

AUGUSTUS AND HIS **SMILE**
CATHERINE RAYNER

Come home to great books
from Little Tiger Press

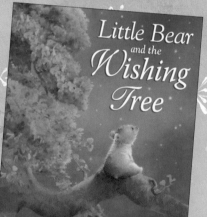

STEVE SMALLMAN
THE LAMB WHO CAME FOR DINNER
JOËLLE DREIDEMY

Little Bear and the *Wishing Tree*
Norbert Landa · Simon Mendez

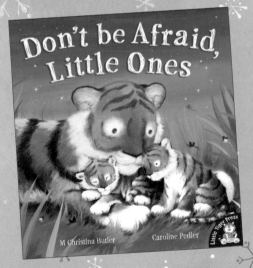

Don't be Afraid, Little Ones
M Christina Butler · Caroline Pedler

For information regarding any of the above titles
or for our catalogue, please contact us:
Little Tiger Press, 1 The Coda Centre,
189 Munster Road, London SW6 6AW
Tel: 020 7385 6333 Fax: 020 7385 7333
E-mail: info@littletiger.co.uk
www.littletigerpress.com